HELLO

I'm Ger

As I'm sure you know from my brother's bestselling novels, I'm a special correspondent for *The Rodent's Gazette*, Mouse Island's most famous newspaper. Unlike my 'fraidy mouse brother, I absolutely adore traveling, having adventures, and meeting rodents from all around the world!

The adventure I want to tell you about begins at Mouseford Academy, the school I went to when I was a young mouseling. I had such a great experience there as a student that I came back to teach a journalism class.

When I returned as a grown mouse, I met five really special students: Colette, Nicky, Pamela, Paulina, and Violet. You could hardly imagine five more different mouselings, but they became great friends right away. And they liked me so much that they decided to name their group after me: the Thea Sisters! I was so touched by that, I decided to write about their adventures. So turn the page to read a fabumouse adventure about the

THEA SISTERS!

Colette

She has a passion for clothing and style, especially anything pink. When she grows up, she wants to be a fashion editor.

Paulina

Cheerful and kind, she loves traveling and meeting rodents from all over the world. She has a magic touch when it comes to technology.

Violet

She's the bookworm of the group, and she loves learning. She enjoys classical music and dreams of becoming a famous violinist.

THE THEA SISTERS

Nicky

She comes from Australia and is very enthusiastic about sports and nature. She loves being outside and is always ready to get up and go!

Pamela

She is a great mechanic: Give her a screwdriver and she'll fix anything! She loves pizza, which she eats every day, and she loves to cook.

Do you want to help the Thea Sisters in this new adventure? It's not hard — just follow the clues!

When you see this magnifying glass, pay attention: It means there's an important clue on the page. Each time one appears, we'll review the clues so we don't miss anything.

**ARE YOU READY?
A NEW MYSTERY AWAITS!**

Geronimo Stilton

Thea Stilton
AND THE
NIAGARA SPLASH

Scholastic Inc.

Copyright © 2016 by Edizioni Piemme S.p.A., Palazzo Mondadori, Via Mondadori 1, 20090 Segrate, Italy. International Rights © Atlantyca S.p.A. English translation © 2018 by Atlantyca S.p.A.

The publisher does not have any control over and does not assume any responsibility for author or third-party websites or their content.

GERONIMO STILTON and THEA STILTON names, characters, and related indicia are copyright, trademark, and exclusive license of Atlantyca S.p.A. All rights reserved. The moral right of the author has been asserted. Based on an original idea by Elisabetta Dami. www.geronimostilton.com

Published by Scholastic Inc., *Publishers since 1920,* 557 Broadway, New York, NY 10012. SCHOLASTIC and associated logos are trademarks and/or registered trademarks of Scholastic Inc.

Stilton is the name of a famous English cheese. It is a registered trademark of the Stilton Cheese Makers' Association. For more information, go to www.stiltoncheese.com.

No part of this publication may be reproduced, stored in a retrieval system, or transmitted in any form or by any means, electronic, mechanical, photocopying, recording, or otherwise, without written permission of the copyright holder. For information regarding permission, please contact: Atlantyca S.p.A., Via Leopardi 8, 20123 Milan, Italy; e-mail foreignrights@atlantyca.it, www.atlantyca.com.

This book is a work of fiction. Names, characters, places, and incidents are either the product of the author's imagination or are used fictitiously, and any resemblance to actual persons, living or dead, business establishments, events, or locales is entirely coincidental.

ISBN 978-1-338-21528-1

Text by Thea Stilton
Original title *Missione Niagara*
Cover by Caterina Giorgetti (design) and Flavio Ferron (color)
Illustrations by Barbara Pellizzari and Flavio Ferron
Graphics by Chiara Cebraro

Special thanks to Kathryn McKeon
Translated by Andrea Schaffer
Interior design by Becky James

10 9 8 7 6 5 4 3 2 1   18 19 20 21 22

Printed in the U.S.A.   40
First printing 2018

SURPRISE!

It was the crack of dawn at Mouseford Academy. The sun was beginning to come up on the HORIZON, painting the sky a fabumouse shade of pink. It was a special day for the students at Mouseford: **Winter vacation had begun!**

Even though there were no classes on that **cold** morning, someone had set the alarm clock . . .

RIIIIIIIING!

"Time to get up, Pam," whispered Colette, silencing the sound of the alarm clock and sitting up in bed. "Pam?"

How strange. Her roommate's bed was empty.

"Two steps ahead of you, Coco," Pam said with a grin, appearing at the foot of Colette's bed, fully dressed. "I've been up FUREVER! I just could not stop thinking about the surprise breakfast we planned for Nicky and Paulina. And the more I thought about it, the hungrier I got!"

Colette chuckled. "Well, this room does smell delicious!"

She got dressed quickly as Pam pulled a wicker basket tied with a bow out of the closet. Then the two girls filled the basket with the muffins they had bought the night before at the Daisy Bakery.

"It's perfect, let's go get Violet," Colette announced.

Just then, there was a gentle knock on the door.

"Wow!" Pam said after opening it to discover her friend Violet. "Sorry I sound **surprised**, Vi. I just can't believe you woke up this early. We all know how you hate getting up in the morning. Did you bring the supplies?"

I'm not a morning mouse!

4

"**TA-DA!**" said Violet, holding open her canvas bag. Inside was a large thermos of **HOT** water and a tin filled with various types of tea. "I know I'm not a morning mouse, so I planned ahead. I packed everything last night, and all I had to do was roll out of bed and get dressed this morning."

Quietly, the three friends scurried down the hall to Nicky and Paulina's room.

But when they **knocked** on the door, they were surprised to discover Nicky and Paulina were already up and dressed.

"Why are you guys awake?" squeaked Colette. "Your flight to **Canada** doesn't leave for hours!"

"We were too excited to sleep!" explained Paulina. "But why are you three awake?"

Pam held up the basket filled with **whisker-licking-good** breakfast treats and announced, "We're here to surprise our friends who are leaving for Canada . . .

with a yummy BREAKFAST!"

ALWAYS TOGETHER!

Pam passed around the basket of muffins while Violet poured cups of steaming tea. Then the five mouselings sat down together to enjoy their delicious breakfast.

"I propose that the 'going-away breakfast' becomes one of our traditions!" announced Nicky, nibbling on her blueberry muffin.

"I second that motion!" nodded Paulina happily.

Though both girls were looking forward to their trip, they were going to miss hanging out with the other Thea Sisters.

Violet poured another round of tea as the mouselets chattered excitedly about their upcoming adventure. The two friends were going to Toronto to attend the launch of the city's first guided **bird-watching** tour.

"I can't wait to get there! Canada is supposed to be so beautiful!" gushed Paulina.

"And I can't wait to finally meet **Adele** in person!" added Nicky, grinning.

Adele was a young rodent the two friends met when they joined an environmentalist group online called the **Green Mice**. She lived in **Toronto** and was looking for volunteers to organize a bird-watching tour in the city. Paulina and Nicky loved the idea, so they contacted Adele and had been working **virtually** with her ever since.

"When you think about it, it seems pretty incredible that you were able to **organize** everything while you were here and she was in **Canada**," noted Violet.

"I know, right?" agreed Nicky.

The mouselings had their first **virtual meeting** with Adele at the end of the summer. She was so easy to talk to, and her enthusiasm for **bird-watching** was infectious!

In the months since that first meeting, the mouselings had exchanged long emails and had set up Friday night video-conference sessions. Together, they had figured out the tour route through the city, **highlighting** all the different species of birds to be viewed at each stop. They had also created C O L O R F U L flyers advertising the event and put together **SIGNS** they planned on setting up along the route.

"Adele is awesome," squeaked Paulina. "I can't believe we have become such good **friends** in such a short time."

"And soon we'll get to meet her whole family, since we're staying at her house," added Nicky.

Just then, Paulina glanced at her watch and jumped up. "Oh my goodmouse!" she squeaked. "We better get moving or we'll miss our flight!"

"Don't worry. I can drive," offered Pamela, shaking her car keys.

Before the mouselings left for the airport, Colette had one more surprise in store for her friends. She pulled out five COLORFUL wool hats from her bag. Each hat was decorated with a pom-pom in the shape of a heart.

"Coco, these are fantastic!" laughed Nicky. The girls all put on their hats and modeled for each other.

"You two will wear yours in Toronto,

and we'll wear ours at Mouseford," explained Colette. "So, even if we are *far away*, it will almost be like we are all together!"

CANADA is the second MOST EXPANSIVE country (after Russia), and the border that separates it from the United States is the longest in the world! Even though it is an extremely vast country, it is home to only a SMALL PART of the world's population.

Canada is a MULTICULTURAL nation: Its population, in fact, has both European (mostly British and French) and Asian origins. In addition, in the most northern regions, there are some INUIT populations.

Canada is a BILINGUAL country; English and French are the two official languages.

Continent: **North America**
Capital: **Ottawa**
Official Languages:
English and French
Money:
Canadian Dollar

WELCOME TO TORONTO!

Nicky and Paulina couldn't wait to get to **Canada**. They spent most of the flight chattering excitedly and staring out the window at the changing landscape.

Finally, after many hours, the city of Toronto appeared.

"Look at the snow!" exclaimed Nicky, admiring the **frosted** landscape that was getting closer and closer.

Paulina grinned, pulling out the **WOOL HAT** Colette had given her and tugging it over her ears. "Coco will be happy to know that her gift came in handy!" she squeaked.

Even though there was a **crowd** at the airport terminal, it didn't take the Thea

Sisters long to find their friend. Adele's huge smile and twinkling eyes lit up the room.

"You're here!" she cried, *running* to hug each of them. "I can't believe we are FINALLY meeting in person!"

The friends had so much to talk about, but there was no time. The opening ceremony

You're here!

for the bird-watching tour was about to begin. Adele led the way.

"The start of the tour is not far from here," she explained after the friends had all piled into her car. Nicky pressed

Good job!

her nose to the GLASS, taking in the scenery.

Before long, the mouselings arrived at the edge of a park.

"Here we are, right on **time**!" said Adele, parking in a nearby lot.

Adele introduced the Thea Sisters to a few other members of the GREEN MICE, then turned to address the crowd. There

There are various paths . . .

were rodents alone and in pairs and lots of families with small mouselings. Many of the mice had brought their own binoculars.

"I'm so happy to see everyone! I am honored to welcome you all to Toronto's first bird-watching tour!" Adele squeaked excitedly. "Before we get started with our tour, I'd like to thank my dear friends from the Green Mice, Nicky and Paulina, for helping me organize this event!"

Adele went on to explain about the different trails they would be taking in order to view a variety of bird species that populated the city. These included **mourning doves**, blue jays, **cardinals**, and swans.

Soon, the tour took off winding through the city. There were so many birds to see . . . and hear! In fact, Adele and the Thea Sisters identified many of the birds by their unique songs! Everyone seemed to be enjoying themselves. They pointed at the birds in the trees and whispered to each other in awe.

When the guided tour was over, everyone CLAPPED.

"You were great, Adele!" Nicky and Paulina gushed after the crowd left. They looked enthusiastically at the photos they had taken.

The Thea Sisters sent some of the photos to the mouselets back home. They were so excited about all the birds they had seen, and they were ready to explore more trails. But Adele had other plans. She suggested they head back to her house to unpack and relax.

"Don't worry. We'll have plenty of time to go bird-watching over the next few days," Adele assured her friends. "But for

now I thought we could **warm** up with some tea back at my house. Then we could do a sightseeing tour of the city."

Nicky grinned as Paulina squeaked,

"THAT SOUNDS GREAT!"

A ROOM FIT FOR FIVE MICE!

Adele lived with her family in a town house not far from the center of Toronto.

"Sorry no one is here to welcome you," Adele apologized when they arrived. "My parents are at work, and my brother, Liam, is taking classes at the UNIVERSITY," she explained, pointing to a framed picture of her family. Then she led Nicky and Paulina up the STAIRS to the room where they would be staying.

Upstairs, the attic had been turned into a beautiful, spacious room, complete with three large sofas, cozy chairs, a bookcase filled with books, and sunny skylights.

"Wow! This room is *perfect*!" commented Nicky.

Wow!

"We like to have guests, so we remodeled the **ATTIC** to host friends who come visit us," said Adele with a smile.

In fact, the room had two SLEEPER couches and three chairs that transformed into single beds. "This room can actually sleep FIVE rodents," Adele said.

"It would be perfect for all the THEA SISTERS," noted Paulina with a laugh.

Of course, Adele had heard all about the other Thea Sisters. The five friends from **MOUSEFORD ACADEMY** seemed to do everything together.

"I would **love** to meet your friends someday," exclaimed Adele.

"Well . . . what are we waiting for? Come on, I'll **introduce you**!" responded Paulina, pulling out her tablet from her backpack. A few minutes later, Colette, Violet, and Pamela appeared on the screen.

When the video call was **over**, Adele squeaked, "Your friends are great! You have to bring them with you the next time you come to **Toronto**!"

"We will," agreed Nicky, pulling on her jacket. "But now let's go explore the city!"

WALKING AROUND THE CITY

Since it was almost lunchtime, Adele knew exactly where to take her friends to begin their tour of **Toronto**.

"Welcome to ST. LAWRENCE MARKET!" she announced, pointing to an imposing REDBRICK building.

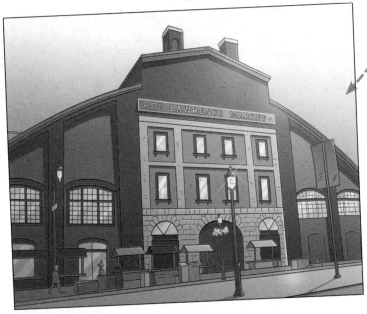

ST. LAWRENCE MARKET opened back in the 1800s and is known today as one of the world's greatest markets. It is made up of more than 120 specialty vendors who sell everything from **fresh fruits** and vegetables to meats, **FISH**, baked goods, **antiques**, and crafts.

"This place is **amazing**!" declared Paulina as the friends wandered through the colorful stalls, checking out the merchandise.

For lunch, the mouselings settled on cheesy gourmet **BAGEL SANDWICHES**. Afterward, they left the market and continued strolling through the city. There was so much to see in Toronto!

Suddenly, Adele had a fabumouse idea. "Who wants to get a real **BIRD'S-EYE** view of the city?" she asked Nicky and Paulina.

"But how can we do that?" Nicky asked, puzzled.

Adele giggled. She put an arm around her new friend and pointed to a building that towered over the highest skyscrapers. "See that building? It's the **Canadian National Tower**. It's one of our city's most popular tourist destinations. It has the most incredible views!"

Adele explained that the tower stood at nearly **TWO THOUSAND FEET**. It contained three restaurants, a state-of-the-art theater, and a gift shop. "And to get to the top, we'll ride the GLASS ELEVATOR that takes only fifty-eight seconds!" she added.

A few minutes later, the two Mouseford students stood **speechless** on the

observation deck of the tower.

"**Breathtaking!**" Paulina observed, snapping pictures.

Later, when the mouselings returned to street level, a cold wind RUFFLED their fur.

"I guess it's true what they say about winter in Canada," Nicky observed, pulling the neck of her jacket up to her ears. "It sure is cold here."

"Don't worry. I'll show you how we can walk without worrying about the cold," Adele said, leading her friends DOWN into what looked like a subway entrance.

Nicky and Paulina soon found themselves in a type of underground city.

Adele unbuttoned her coat and explained, "This is THE PATH, our underground walkway. It's eighteen miles long and lets us get where we're going without freezing our tails off. Plus, there are lots of stores, restaurants, and even MUSEUMS down here."

Walking in the **warmth** made the hours fly by. Finally, they were ready to return to the street.

"I thought we would make one last stop before going home," said Adele, stopping in front of a large ROUND building. "You can't say that you have been to Canada if you haven't gotten to know our national sport . . . ICE HOCKEY!"

GO, STORMS!

Adele led the mouselings through the deserted hallways of the **ice rink** until they emerged at the top of a **TALL** set of bleachers. The friends **scurried** to the edge of the rink, where a team was practicing.

"This is great! I always dreamed of seeing an **ICE HOCKEY** game!" exclaimed Nicky, hugging Adele.

"Well, this is only a practice," explained Adele. "But we can go to a **REAL** game. It's one of the most important

ICE HOCKEY

The sport of ice hockey began in the mid-1800s in the eastern parts of Canada. James G. Creighton of Nova Scotia organized the very first hockey game played on a rink of ice with a "flat circular piece of wood" known as a PUCK.

games for the CHAMPIONSHIP."

Right then, the mouselings heard a loud whistle. The coach had called a five-minute break for the players.

Paulina and Nicky watched as one of the players took off his helmet and glanced in their direction. Paulina furrowed her brow. "How strange. I feel like I've seen that player somewhere before," she squeaked, shaking her head.

"Me too," Nicky added, trying to figure out where the mouselings might have met.

At that moment, the player skated over to them.

"You must be Nicky and Paulina!" he said, smiling. "It's so great to finally meet you!"

"But how —" Paulina began to say, when suddenly she was interrupted by Nicky.

"Hey, I know who you are! You're Liam,

Adele's brother!" Nicky exclaimed. "We saw P I C T U R E S of you back at the house!"

Liam grinned. He explained how his sister had shown him pictures of her new friends on the Green Mice website.

"Consider the **Mystery** solved," chuckled Paulina.

You must be Nicky and Paulina! It's nice to meet you!

Adele turned to her brother. "Is **JUSTIN** here today?" she asked.

"Of course." Liam nodded, pointing to the other side of the rink. "He's **DOWN** there with Elliott, talking to the coach."

Nicky and Paulina learned that Justin was Liam's **best friend** and possibly the next captain of the Storms, the university **HOCKEY** team that they both played on.

"The other candidate is Elliott. He is still on the ice," explained Liam.

The two players joined the group.

Once they were all together, Nicky said, "Congratulations! We heard that one of you will be the next captain of the **STORMS**!"

Justin and Elliott smiled. The coach was due to make his decision before their next big game, which would be against the **THUNDER**.

"May the **best** mouse win!" squeaked Paulina.

"Then he'll win!" responded Justin and Elliott in unison, POINTING at each other.

Paulina whispered to Nicky, "Did you notice that when Justin arrived, Adele got really quiet? She hardly squeaked!"

Nicky nodded in agreement. For a mouseling as outgoing as Adele, it sure seemed strange.

The two Thea Sisters decided there was only one way to find out what was going on. As soon as practice restarted, they asked her.

"Oh, how **embarrassing**!" exclaimed Adele, **blushing** furiously at the mention of Justin's name. With a sigh, she confessed to her new friends that she had a crush on her brother's teammate.

Ahem . . .

"He's so **NICE** and thoughtful. I'd love to ask him to go bird-watching with us, but whenever I'm around him, I can't seem to be able to put two words together," she admitted.

"Hey, it's nothing to be

embarrassed about!" Nicky assured her friend. "It's normal to feel **shy** sometimes."

"That's true," agreed Paulina. "But think of it this way, he may think you're **NICE**, too. And he would probably have fun on the bird-watching tour."

Adele felt a little **surge** of excitement. Maybe her friends were right. That's it. She would find the **COURAGE** to ask Justin.

Outside, after practice was over, Adele grabbed one of the bird-watching **FLYERS** from her purse.

"Um, Justin, I —" she began nervously. But before she could finish, a **LOUD** voice interrupted her.

"Well, well, well, look who's here! The worst players on the ice!" snorted a big mouse with **red** hair. He was carrying a sports bag with a huge **T** embroidered on it.

"Rob! It's always nice to see you!" Justin said without **flinching**.

"We'll see how nice it is next week when the **THUNDER** take your team to the bottom of the league!" retorted Rob.

"**WOW!** He was so rude!" observed Nicky. "Who was that?"

Justin explained that Rob is the captain of the THUNDER, the Storms' rival team. The two teams would play against each other in the big CHAMPIONSHIP game. Apparently, Rob has a habit of picking on his opponents before games to make them nervous.

"I really don't understand how you don't BLOW UP at him, Justin," Liam commented. "He makes me so mad!"

Justin shrugged his shoulders. "Rob loves to brag a lot, but I don't let it bother me. I'd rather just show him how great our team is when we get on the ice," he said with a wide grin. "I bet old Rob won't be bragging then!"

WiNTER WONDERLAND WALK!

The next morning, Paulina and Nicky woke up to the most delicious aroma. Quickly, the two friends got dressed and followed the MOUTHWATERING scent down the stairs all the way to the kitchen.

"Good morning!" Adele greeted them, placing a stack of steaming pancakes in the center of the table.

"**Pancakes!**" exclaimed Paulina, eyeing the inviting plate of golden flapjacks.

"With a breakfast like this, it's

impossible to not be **hungry**!" squeaked Nicky.

The Thea Sisters eagerly sat down to eat as Adele passed around a small bottle of **maple syrup**. Before long, the group was joking and laughing and **gobbling** up the yummy pancakes.

"Save some for me!" Liam joked, joining the group. In the blink of an eye, he scarfed down three pancakes, then turned to his sister. "So what **PLANS** do you have for today?" he asked.

Adele stared out the window at the **BRIGHT** sunlight. "Well, since it's not snowing, I thought I could show them the **Toronto Islands**," she suggested.

"Great idea!" nodded Liam. "We can wear snowshoes and hike through the snowy **PARKS**."

"We?" asked Adele.

"Yes, I don't have class today, so I am officially inviting myself!" announced Liam, smiling cheerfully. Then, taking out his **smartphone**, he began to type a message. "I'll ask Justin if he wants to come with us."

TORONTO ISLANDS

They are the SMALL ISLANDS IN LAKE ONTARIO that are part of the city of Toronto. Reachable by ferry in only ten minutes from the center of the city, these islands are a NATURAL OASIS made up of TREE-FILLED parks, SANDY beaches, and award-winning GARDENS. And to cut down on pollution, no cars are allowed!

Justin was definitely up for the trip. He loved doing anything outdoors, and it was a beautiful day to spend on the islands.

The mouselings met at the pier and hopped aboard one of the three ferries headed for the islands. Ten minutes later, they arrived. Strapping on SNOWSHOES, the group took off, excited to explore the snow-covered trails. What an amazing WINTER WONDERLAND! Nicky and Paulina spent hours snapping pictures of the breathtaking views. Finally, after a cup of delicious **hot chocolate** at an island café, they returned to the mainland.

"Wow! That was so amazing! What should we do next?!" squeaked Nicky, feeling totally energized by the trip. Being out in the cold fresh air and exercising were two of Nicky's most favorite things to do.

Justin laughed. Nicky looked like she was ready to run a marathon. "I have an idea. How about we go over to the ICE RINK and you can WATCH us try some plays," he suggested.

Nicky's eyes shone. Justin's idea was good, but she had an even better one. The only time she had tried to play hockey was on the FROZEN LAKE on Whale Island. Now would be her chance to skate on a real ice rink!

"Okay, Justin," she agreed. "But I don't want to watch. I want to play!"

Justin and Liam grinned. "Okay," they said in unison as everyone laughed.

"Don't laugh!" Nicky scolded the group,

pretending to be offended. "Girls can play! Besides, I'm not going to miss an opportunity to play with two real **Canadian** hockey players!"

PACK YOUR BAGS!

The next day, Nicky and Paulina had decided to begin the day with a **video call** to their friends back at Mouseford to update them on their Canadian trip.

"So you played HOCKEY with Liam and Justin? On a real rink?" asked Colette, **smiling** at her friends through the screen on Paulina's tablet.

"Exactly!" confirmed Nicky. "We did a few exchanges and some **face-offs**,* and I took a few shots on goal."

"Hey! I want to SEE a photo of our Nicky on the ice!" exclaimed Pam.

Paulina quickly found a PICTURE and sent it over to her friends at Mouseford.

"She looks like a real PRO," Pam exclaimed.

*During the game, two opposing players face each other and try to get hold of the puck before their opponent.

Nicky played hockey!

"So what are you doing today?" asked Colette.

"We really haven't decided . . ." Nicky began. A sharp dinging sound signaled an incoming message on her smartphone.

At the same time, Paulina's phone began to

We want a photo!

buzz, too. "Looks like Liam, Justin, and Adele have included us in a group chat," she observed.

A minute later, Adele **POKED** her head in the door. "Sorry to bother you, but do you two know what Justin and Liam are talking about?" she squeaked.

"What are they talking about?"

asked Pam and Colette excitedly from the video call.

Nicky and Paulina chuckled. Oh, how they missed their friends at **MOUSEFORD**!

Adele smiled at the SCREEN, including

the three other Thea Sisters as she filled them all in on the details. "Well, they say they want us to pack our bags because we're going on a **surprise** weekend away!"

Even though they weren't in Canada, Violet and Colette **clapped** in delight. "This is so exciting!" squeaked Violet.

"Hurry up and pack!" Colette urged her

friends. "We can't wait to hear about your adventure!"

Waving good-bye to their friends at Mouseford, Paulina, Nicky, and Adele packed their backpacks. As promised, Liam and Justin were waiting outside.

"So now will you tell us *where we're going*?" asked Paulina as the group piled into Liam's car.

"I know. Let's play a game. You can each ask a question. Then we'll see who can guess our **surprise** destination!" Justin suggested.

"Okay," said Adele as the car turned onto a highway. "How far away is it?"

"About an hour and a half," responded Liam.

"**North** or **south**?" asked Nicky.

"South," said Justin.

"*I know!*" exclaimed Paulina as they drove by a huge blue sign confirming her guess.

"We're going to . . . NIAGARA FALLS!"

THE THREE WATERFALLS

NIAGARA FALLS is located on the border between Canada and the United States and is a popular tourist destination. The water begins in the Upper Great Lakes, and the river is believed to be twelve thousand years old. Niagara Falls is made up of three waterfalls: Horseshoe Falls, American Falls, and Bridal Veil Falls.

HORSESHOE FALLS is named after its semicircular or horseshoe-like shape. It is found on the Canadian side of the border.

AMERICAN WATERFALLS and BRIDAL VEIL FALLS are both on the American side. Separating the Canadian waterfalls from the American waterfalls is a small island called Goat Island.

ARE YOU READY TO LOSE?

As the friends sped down the road toward the falls, the excitement in the car grew. Of course, the Thea Sisters had heard about the beauty of Niagara Falls, but they could hardly believe they were about to see them fur real! Paulina pulled out her smartphone and began reading aloud about the history of the falls and other fun facts.

"Can you believe daredevils have actually walked tightropes over the falls and plunged down in barrels?" Paulina remarked.

"Not my idea of fun!" Adele said with a laugh. "I'll stick to bird-watching!"

The group was still laughing when they

arrived at the falls. Not wanting to waste any time, the mouselings agreed to head to the falls as soon as they had checked into the **HOTEL**.

"Let's put our **bags** in our rooms, and then we can meet in the lobby," Liam suggested, leading the way down a **long** hallway.

"Okay, it looks like Justin and I are in room 102 and —" But before Liam could finish his sentence, a loud **obnoxious** voice interrupted him.

"Well, look who's here: Liam and Justin!" snorted a rodent Nicky and Paulina soon recognized.

"**Rob?**" exclaimed Adele, surprised to discover not only that the captain of the Thunder was on a trip to **NIAGARA FALLS** with his friends but also that he had a room in the same hotel!

"Hey, Justin, shouldn't you be home practicing?" Rob asked.

Justin shook his head and laughed, causing Rob to **SCOWL** and walk off. It was no fun **PICKING** on someone if they didn't get upset!

"That Rob is so **RUDE**!" squeaked Paulina.

Rob?!

Are you ready to lose?

"But Justin showed him!" Adele added, giving Justin a **shy** smile.

Now that Rob the **bully** was gone, the mouselings continued on with their plans. Racing to their rooms, they threw down their bags and took off for the falls.

"Wow!" squeaked Nicky when they arrived at the park surrounding the falls. The water

Wow!   Incredible!   Amazing!   Fabumouse!

CRASHED down with such force, it sent up a fine sparkling white mist.

"Incredible!" exclaimed Paulina, pulling out her phone to take a picture.

The crashing waterfalls and rising mist set against the snowy landscape gave the whole place an enchanted feeling. It was true what Nicky had read on her phone. Visiting Niagara Falls was like entering a magical fairy-tale world!

The time flew by, and before long, the sun had begun to set, turning the sky a brilliant ORANGE and PINK.

"We better head back to the hotel," Liam suggested. "But tonight we can catch a cool fireworks show here!"

The hotel felt warm and welcoming after their day outside in the cold. Adele couldn't wait to make a nice cup of tea with the

teakettle she had spotted in their room.

But as the mouselings headed down the hallway toward their rooms, Adele stopped in her tracks. She pointed to a piece of P A P E R attached to Justin and Liam's door.

It read: **LOSERS INSIDE!**

"Now Rob is really getting annoying!" scoffed Liam.

Justin nodded. Without a word, he *RIPPED* the note off the door, **MARCHED** down the hall to Rob's room, and knocked.

When the door opened, Rob faced him and sneered. "Yes? How can I help you?"

"You know very well," responded Justin, placing the paper in his paw. "We've had enough of your *insults*!"

"Poor **STORMS**," said Rob, pretending to **CRY**. "They're so sensitive."

"I'm warning you: Leave us alone. We'll see who the real losers are at the **Game**!" said Justin, turning to leave.

"That's right, run away!" scoffed Rob.

MISSING
MOUSELING

Back in their room, Nicky and Paulina grabbed the tablet so they could **video-chat** with their friends back at Mouseford. They couldn't wait to fill them in on all the amazing sights they had seen that day. Too bad the day had to end with an **obnoxious** encounter with Rob, the captain of the **THUNDER**.

"He sounds pawsitively awful!" observed Colette.

Nicky nodded. "He's exactly the type of **ATHLETE** I don't like. Competition on the field is not enough, so he picks on his rivals, trying to make them feel **inferior**!"

Paulina snorted. "I really hope we don't

run into him anymore while we are here!"

"Well, if you do, try not to let his **RUDE** words ruin your trip," advised Violet.

"We will try." Adele nodded, not **completely** convinced.

Once they had said good-bye to their

We need to ignore him!

It's not easy . . .

friends at **MOUSEFORD,** the three mouselings quickly got ready to meet Liam and Justin in the lobby of the hotel.

"This is so exciting! I've never seen a waterfall at night!" squeaked Paulina, clapping her paws eagerly in anticipation.

Nicky, too, was so thrilled she could hardly stand still.

"Let's go, then! The show is about to begin!" replied Liam.

The mouselings proceeded along a path decorated with rows of GLITTERING LIGHTS attached to the terrace that FACED the Horseshoe Falls. Once they got there, all five of their jaws dropped as they took in the stunning panoramic view before them. In the darkness, the show of lights lit up the roaring falls in all the colors of the rainbow.

As the friends watched the display, Adele pulled Nicky and Paulina aside. "Guess what? I decided that after the fireworks show, I am going to ask Justin to come to the **bird-watching** tour," she whispered.

"Great idea!" exclaimed Nicky.

At that moment, the first **firework** exploded in the sky and the crowd erupted in a chorus of **ooooohs!** and **aaaaahs!** What a sight!

It wasn't until the show ended that the friends realized that someone in their group was missing . . .

"Where did Justin go?" asked Nicky, looking around.

Liam **FURROWED** his brow. "I don't know. When the show began, he was next to me, but then . . . I **LOST** sight of him."

"Maybe he went off to take some photos," guessed Paulina.

The group waited a few minutes for their friend to return, then tried his cell. There was no response. **HOW STRANGE.** Finally, they decided to return to the **HOTEL** to wait.

"This is so **weird**," Liam said as soon as he set foot in his room. "Justin's backpack isn't here; he **disappeared** with all of his things!"

"But why?" asked Adele, perplexed. "Where could he have gone?"

Right at that moment, they all heard a beeping sound. It was a message on the group **chat** that the guys had created for the trip.

Since the rest of the group was all together, the message could only be from one person . . . **JUSTIN**!

Snowstorm Swirling!

The following morning, the return trip to Toronto was very different from the trip from Toronto. Nicky, Paulina, Adele, and Liam spoke very little, each staring at the SNOW that fell lightly on the windshield of the car.

No one had the COURAGE to say it, but it was clear that everyone was thinking the same thing. The way Justin left was really strange!

When they got home, Nicky, Paulina, and Adele decided to stay indoors and watch a movie while Liam headed off to practice.

"Hey, Big Brother, how did it go today?" asked Adele when Liam returned later and joined the girls in the living room.

"I don't know," he responded, **SHRUGGING** his shoulders.

"What do you mean?" asked Paulina, giving him a puzzled look. "Did something happen with that **bully** Rob again?"

Liam shook his head. "No, it's not about

Rob. It's just that **JUSTIN** wasn't at practice today!"

The three mouselings exchanged a perplexed look.

"And that's not all," continued Liam. "I tried calling him a few times, but he isn't answering his cell phone. And then at practice I talked to a bunch of my teammates and other friends, and *not one of them* was in NIAGARA FALLS this weekend," concluded Liam with a worried tone.

"So who did Justin leave with last NIGHT?" asked Nicky.

"And where is he now?" added Paulina.

"I have no idea," sighed Liam. "But this **situation** doesn't seem right at all!"

"Wait a minute," Adele said, taking the **television remote** and turning up the volume on the television. "Listen!"

"The satellite data tell us that a strong **storm** is arriving within the next few hours that will impact the Niagara Falls region particularly hard," the **newscaster** was saying.

On the screen, the newscaster pointed to an image of a strong, **swirling** snowstorm headed for the falls. "So if you find yourself

A strong snowstorm is arriving....

in those parts, we recommend that you stay indoors if possible. If it isn't an emergency, please stay safe and warm inside your homes until the storm has passed."

REINFORCEMENTS ARE COMING!

Adele, Liam, and the two Thea Sisters spent the **EVENING** trying to contact Justin but had no luck.

The more time that passed, the more worried they became, wondering if their friend was stuck in **NIAGARA FALLS** at the exact time a **blizzard** was due to hit.

"I just don't understand it. He's still **UNREACHABLE**," announced Liam after trying to call Justin for what seemed like the **MILLIONTH** time.

Meanwhile, Paulina was staring at the message Justin had sent. Something didn't **add up**. She turned to her friends. "You know, I keep reading this **message**, and

How strange . . .

even if I don't know Justin very well, I have to say, it doesn't **SOUND** like the other messages he sent!" she squeaked.

"You're right," said Adele. "Justin doesn't usually sound so formal, and he always uses a lot of exclamation points and funny faces, but . . ."

"But this message is **FLAT** and impersonal," Liam agreed.

CLUE!
JUSTIN'S MESSAGE IS VERY DIFFERENT FROM THE MESSAGES THAT HE USUALLY WRITES. WHY?

The room fell silent until a ring coming from Paulina's tablet made everyone jump. It wasn't a call from Justin, though; it was a **video call** from Mouseford. Paulina hit a key to answer and Pam's voice immediately filled the room. "**Hey, Sisters! How's it going?**"

"We're good," Nicky mumbled.

"Okay, so what's going on?" asked Colette. "We've been writing you messages all day and you haven't responded. What's wrong?"

Nicky and Paulina exchanged a glance. Why didn't they think of **consulting** the other Thea Sisters sooner? After all, together the Thea Sisters had solved lots of **mysteries!**

The girls quickly described everything that had happened so far, beginning with Justin's sudden disappearance at the fireworks and ending with his strange **text message**.

"That does sound really odd," observed Colette.

"I know, right?" agreed Paulina. "I mean, it's almost like Justin has disappeared into thin air! No one has seen him since that **NIGHT** at the falls."

"**SHOOT!**" snorted Pamela in frustration. "I wish we could help you solve this **mystery**, but we're so far away. I'm not sure what we can do."

"I have an idea!" exclaimed Adele, joining Nicky and Paulina on the call. "Why don't you mouselings come to **Toronto**? We've got plenty of room and we could sure use your help!"

On the screen, Violet, Pamela, and Colette squeaked.

"Are you sure?" asked Pam, hoping the answer was **Yes**.

Adele assured the mouselings that she was more than sure. "Together, we'll be a **super team**!" she cried.

Colette, Pamela, and Violet looked at one another for a second and then each broke

Come to Toronto!

into a **wide** grin. They didn't even have to SQUEAK to know what they were all thinking.

"We'd love to come!" exclaimed Violet, her eyes sparkling with enthusiasm. "We'll go pack our bags right now."

THE CURIOUS CALL

"There they are!" squeaked Nicky the next day as Colette, Pamela, and Violet **exited** the airport.

The Thea Sisters embraced one another **warmly**, thrilled to be together again. And when Paulina introduced Adele, the whole group SWEPT her up in one massive group **hug**!

"Thanks for inviting us!" Colette gushed, squeezing Adele's paw.

"I'm so happy you agreed to come. I just wish you were here on **vacation**, and not because one of our friends has **mysteriously** disappeared," sighed Adele.

Grabbing their bags, the Thea Sisters

piled into Adele's car and headed for Justin's **COLLEGE DORM**, where Liam was waiting. When they arrived, Liam reported that he had spoken to a number of mouselings who knew Justin. They all said they hadn't seen Justin since he left for **NIAGARA FALLS**.

"**NOW** what do we do?" asked Paulina, shoving her paws in her pockets to keep warm.

"Well, Justin gave me a set of **KEYS** to his room so whenever he goes away I can take care of his aquarium," Liam said, jingling the keys in the air. "I thought we could feed the **FISH** and see if we find any clues in Justin's room."

"Good idea! Let's go!" agreed Colette, following Liam into a large yellow brick building.

The rest of the group trailed after them, walking single file down the narrow hallway that led to Justin's room.

After feeding the fish, the mouselings LOOKED around carefully but didn't notice anything particularly strange.

The room was **clean** and orderly, just as Justin had left it before leaving for the weekend in NIAGARA FALLS.

"I came over to get Justin before going to the falls, and this room pretty much looks the way I **remembered** it. It looks like he hasn't been back here since then," Liam concluded.

Paulina shook her head, staring thoughtfully at the fish *swimming* back and forth in the tank. Even the fish seemed to be looking for Justin. Where could he be?

"I don't get the feeling Justin planned on **staying** away long," observed Violet.

"I agree," added Pamela. "In the picture you sent us, he was only carrying a small backpack."

Then she turned to Liam and said, "It sounds like you and Justin are in touch every day. Even if you are with other friends, he would normally **text** or call to tell you what he's doing, right?"

"Absolutely!" confirmed Liam. "In fact, I'm really starting to think he may be in **trouble** and —"

RIIIIIIIING!

His cell phone interrupted him.

"**IT'S JUSTIN!**" exclaimed Liam, staring with relief at his cell and hitting speakerphone so that his **friends** could listen.

"Liam! 𝓕𝒾𝓃𝒶𝓁𝓁𝓎 I was able to get through!" Justin's voice sounded far away. A loud whooshing sound almost drowned out his words. The

It's him!

Thea Sisters and Adele instinctively gathered around Liam so they could hear better.

"Where are you?" asked Adele.

"We are all **worried** about you!"

"Don't worry. I'm okay," Justin reassured them. "But I need you to COME GET ME. I am —"

Right at that moment, the call started to break up.

"Justin!" called Nicky. "Justin, can you hear us?"

CLUE!

✓ JUSTIN'S VOICE IS INTERRUPTED BECAUSE THERE ISN'T GOOD SERVICE AND BECAUSE OF STRONG WINDS. WHERE IS HE?

Paulina shook her head. "The call dropped!"

They immediately tried to call their friend back, but a prerecorded message told them that once again the cell was out of range.

The group erupted in a collective GROAN. Now how were they supposed to find their friend?

"At least we know Justin is okay," Adele offered, trying to look at the situation positively.

Pamela nodded. Still, she thought, Justin needs our help!

A SURLY SUSPECT

After leaving Justin's DORM, the group decided to talk things over at one of the campus dining halls. Adele, Nicky, and Paulina selected some pastries for the mouselings to share while the others ordered hot drinks. Food and drinks in paw, they settled into a large table.

"Okay, let's reexamine what happened the day that Justin disappeared," proposed Paulina, BLOWING on her cup of cinnamon tea.

"Well, we were together all day, having fun," began Nicky, taking a nibble of her chocolate Nanaimo bar.* "And then, that evening, during the

fireworks show, Justin left without telling anyone," continued Adele.

"And later on, he sent that **strange message**," added Liam.

"Why was it strange?" asked Pamela.

Paulina showed her friends the message Justin had sent the evening he disappeared. Then she showed them the messages he had written before his disappearance.

"Oh, yeah, you're right," nodded Violet. "There is an **ENORMOUSE** difference between these messages!"

Pamela was filled with a **NAGGING** suspicion. "Hmmm . . ." she muttered.

"What are you thinking?" prodded Nicky.

Pam sighed. "I was thinking that the last

message actually seems to be written by **SOMEONE ELSE**!"

The whole table went silent.

Finally, Colette broke the silence. "So if your hypothesis is correct," she squeaked, "it would mean that Justin didn't *LEAVE* you

by his own will, but that he was taken away . . ."

". . . by someone who pretended to be him and sent that **message** so we would think everything was fine!" concluded Adele.

"Yes, but who could it have been?" asked Liam, scratching his head.

The whole thing just didn't make sense. Who would want to keep Justin from returning to **Toronto**?

As the group sat **quietly**, pondering the situation, the door to the dining hall opened and a familiar rodent strode in.

"Don't turn around. **Rob** just came in!" whispered Paulina, keeping her head down so he wouldn't see her.

"Let's hope that he doesn't see us," snorted Liam. "I am definitely not in the **mood** for his insults today!"

The group kept silent.

Luckily, the captain of the THUNDER went right up to the counter and placed his order. Then the strangest thing happened. As Rob was waiting, he looked around the dining hall and seemed to GAZE directly at them. But instead of marching up to Liam and making his usual rude comments, he quickly turned his head and stared straight ahead. When his order was ready, he grabbed the take-out coffee cup and raced through the door.

At the table, Adele, Liam, and the Thea Sisters looked at one another in SHOCK.

"That's the famous Rob? The one who never misses an opportunity to annoy you and your teammates?" Pamela asked Liam, watching the red-haired mouseling as he walked away.

Liam nodded. He explained again how much Rob loved to pick on the **STORMS**.

"**Hey, wait a minute!**" exclaimed Colette. "You said that Rob is the captain of the team called the Thunder, right? And isn't that the team that is competing for **FIRST PLACE** in the **CHAMPIONSHIP** game with the Storms?"

The others **NODDED** in silence.

"And didn't you say that Justin is a really **important** player on the team, so much so that he was being considered for the role of captain of the **STORMS**?" continued Colette.

Again, the friends nodded.

"And isn't the final **CHAMPIONSHIP** game happening in a few days?" continued Colette.

At that moment, Paulina **JUMPED** to her feet and began **waving** her paws in the air as if she just won the cheese lottery! She was

I got it!

so **pumped**, she could hardly get the words out fast enough. "I see where you're going with this!" she squeaked excitedly. "We were just wondering who would be interested in keeping Justin away from **Toronto**. And the answer is . . . Rob!"

CLUES!

1. ROB IS ACTING STRANGE AND SEEMS TO AVOID THE THEA SISTERS AND THEIR FRIENDS.

2. ROB'S TEAM WOULD HAVE AN ADVANTAGE IF JUSTIN WEREN'T ABLE TO PLAY IN THE FINAL.

FOLLOW THAT MOUSE!

Without a second to waste, the Thea Sisters gathered their **jackets** and purses and *raced* out of the dining hall. Liam had practice and Adele had to run an important errand for her parents, so the Thea Sisters were on their own. That was okay with the Mouseford students. They had an **IMPORTANT** mission of their own: to solve the case of the disappearing Justin!

Naturally, they couldn't miss the chance to follow Rob, the number one **suspect**!

"If Rob is involved in the sudden disappearance of Justin, sooner or later he's bound to make a **wrong** move," Paulina said.

"And we'll be right there, ready to **CATCH** him in the act!" concluded Pamela confidently.

So the Thea Sisters found themselves trailing the captain of the **THUNDER** to his house.

Across the street from Rob's house, the five mouselings **HID** behind some bushes.

Thea Sisters on a mission!

"So what do we do now?" asked Violet, PEEKING around the side of the bush so she could see the house.

"Let's hang out here and wait for his next move," proposed Paulina.

It wasn't **long** before Rob emerged from the house. He was DRAGGING a bulky duffel bag behind him.

"What if that isn't hockey equipment in there?" asked Nicky. "I think he's making a run for it."

Violet furrowed her brow. "A few days before an important game? How strange."

In fact, Rob's behavior made less and less sense as the friends watched. He seemed so unsure of himself, not at all like the bully they had witnessed in the dorms. And he kept looking around, almost as if he was afraid to be seen.

"He's **HIDING** something," concluded Pamela. "Don't lose him, Sisters!"

Being careful not to be discovered, the girls followed Rob as he boarded a BUS that brought them to the local airport.

Nicky was right!

"**That way!**" Colette pointed, leading her friends through the crowd of passengers who were *headed* toward Departures.

"There he is! I see him!" squeaked Paulina, pointing at Rob far off in the distance. He

Where is he going? We'll find out!

was standing in line to put his BAG on a flight to Montreal!

"Oh, my goodmouse! He's going to Montreal!" cried Violet.

"Do you think JUSTIN could be there?" asked Nicky.

"I don't know, but we need to find out," insisted Colette.

Paulina, in the meantime, consulted her tablet. "There are still lots of available seats on Rob's flight. What do you think? Should I reserve five TICKETS for us?" she proposed.

"But . . . we don't even have baggage!" objected Colette.

"Rob is acting super suspicious. What if he knows where Justin is? We can't let him get away," argued Pamela.

"You're right," Violet nodded. "Let's go! If

we're lucky, we might come back with Justin!"

With a few CLICKS on her tablet, Paulina purchased the tickets. But before the THEA SISTERS could leave, they had one more thing to do.

"Wait!" said Colette, grabbing Nicky and Paulina and directing them toward a clothing store nearby. "Rob hasn't seen me, Pam, or Violet. But he knows you two! Before we get on the same PLANE, we need to get you each a disguise!"

MOUSE HUNT IN MONTREAL!

Luckily, the disguises Colette found for Nicky and Paulina worked perfectly. The captain of the Thunder didn't seem to **SUSPECT** a thing, even though the **THEA SISTERS** were sitting a few rows behind him on the plane.

"If only this hat were a little smaller," whispered Paulina, tugging the hat over her ears. "I feel like it may fall off if I'm not careful."

"If only your head was a little bigger," giggled Nicky, winking at her friend.

Once they arrived in Montreal, the Thea Sisters continued to **follow** Rob as he moved through the city with his large bag.

Even far away from Toronto, he still seemed to be acting strange and kept glancing around *nervously*.

"Hey, LOOK, he's making a call!" exclaimed Pamela, pointing at the mouseling. He was standing now at a bus stop and squeaking into his cell phone.

"I wonder who he's talking to . . ." said Violet.

"I'm going to find out!" announced Colette.

"**Be careful!**" Pamela warned her, trying not to raise her voice too much.

Colette nodded at her friend

and put in the headphones to her **smartphone**. "Don't worry. Rob doesn't know me. He'll think I am a random mouseling just waiting at the bus stop," she said, smoothing her whiskers.

Colette reached the stop and began to look at the window of a BOOKSTORE, pretending to listen to music.

"That's why she put in her headphones." Paulina smiled. "Rob will think that she can't hear him, so he'll feel free to squeak away."

"You're a genius, Sister!" exclaimed Pamela when Colette returned.

"Did you discover anything INTERESTING?" asked Nicky.

"I didn't hear **MUCH**, because Rob was almost whispering, but I think he was talking to a teammate," explained Colette. "And he told a lie! He said that he would be skipping **PRACTICE** because he has a fever!"

"I knew he was **HIDING** something!" exclaimed Paulina.

Suddenly, the bus appeared at the end of

the street. The Thea Sisters hurried to get on behind Rob. But when the bus stopped again, the mouselings **LOST** sight of their suspect in the **huge** crowd.

"Did you see which way he went?" Pamela asked her friends as soon as she climbed off the bus. No one said a word.

A minute later, the mouseling understood why her friends were speechless. The Thea Sisters had just arrived at the most

INCREDIBLE PLACE!

SPARKLING
SCULPTURES

In the square directly in front of the mouselings stood a spectacular display of dozens and dozens of ICE SCULPTURES!

"What is this place?" breathed Colette, looking around in awe.

"It's an ice-sculpting competition!" exclaimed Paulina, holding up a FLYER she had picked up at the entrance. "Sculptors come from all over Canada to participate."

"It seems like hard work," observed Violet, admiring the SCULPTURES around her.

"Yes, but more important, why would Rob come to an ice-sculpting competition?" Colette wondered aloud.

"Good   question," said Pamela, scanning the crowd around her. "We need to find him, Sisters!"

The friends SPLIT UP so they could cover more ground. Though there were **TONS** of rodents at the event, the friends were hoping Rob's **red hair** might make him stand out a little from the crowd.

"Let's try over there," proposed Paulina, spinning around and accidentally **crashing** into someone behind her.

"Oh, I'm sorry," the mouseling apologized, picking up her hat and **sunglasses** that had fallen on the ground. When she looked up, her mouth dropped open.

The person she had **crashed** into was . . . **Rob**!

"**HEY, I KNOW YOU!**" he exclaimed.

Then, seeing Nicky next to her, added, "And I know you, too! You two are friends with **Liam** and **JUSTIN**!"

"Yes, it's us, and we are here for **JUSTIN**!" the mouselets announced.

As soon as they said the name **JUSTIN**, Rob's face turned almost as red as his hair.

I know you!

Ummm . . .

"Is Justin here? Or Liam? What about the Storms? Or the Thunder?" he squeaked, looking nervously over his shoulder.

"We're looking for Justin," responded Paulina. "The others aren't here . . ."

Rob sighed. "Oh, thank goodmouse!"

Huh? Nicky and Paulina were totally confused.

Just then, Colette, Pamela, and Violet joined their friends.

"Hi, Rob, it's nice to meet you," Pamela introduced herself, smiling.

"We just met your father!" added Violet.

"His father?" asked Nicky, even more confused.

Colette nodded, motioning for her friends to follow her.

THE SECRET CASTLE

Colette led the group through the crowd while Rob followed silently behind them. Passing by **ENORMOUS** sculptured ice swans, delicate angels, and *FIRE-BREATHING* dragons, the Thea Sisters marveled at the breathtaking exhibits. Eventually, Colette stopped in front of a sculpture that was not yet finished. It was a spectacular glittering castle.

"Here we are!" declared Colette, pointing to the castle.

Nicky furrowed her brow. "But what does this sculpture have to do with Justin's disappearance?" she asked.

"Oh, no, it doesn't have anything to do

with that," revealed Colette. "It has to do with Rob being in Montreal." She pointed to a sign next to the statue. It told the story of the artists, who are **FATHER** and son.

"You're a sculptor?" exclaimed Paulina, turning to face the captain of the THUNDER.

Rob nodded, **embarrassed**.

"But why don't you want anyone to know?" asked Colette.

"Well . . . I . . ." Rob hesitated. "I am the captain of one of the **strongest** university teams, and in Toronto everyone thinks I am a real TOUGH mouse. What would everyone think if they knew I like to sculpt castles and mermaids?"

The Thea Sisters looked at one another and smiled.

"See? Even you're laughing!" sighed Rob.

"Oh, but we're not smiling because of the statue you made!" explained Pamela. "We're smiling because you're worried that others will think you're not TOUGH if they know you're an artist. But you're not worried that others think you're a bully!"

Rob lowered his gaze. "I know it's not right, but I want my competitors to FEAR me. That way, I'll have an advantage on the ice," he revealed.

Nicky shook her head. "But no one respects a bully," she said. "If I were you, I'd concentrate on showing the other teams what a great HOCKEY PLAYER you are on the ice."

"Being rude just makes you seem shallow, when in reality you are an artist with a sensitive soul," Violet added. "You'd have a lot more friends if you just showed everyone the real you!"

Rob looked thoughtful, and then he smiled. It was the first **sincere** smile they'd ever seen on him.

"You're right," he agreed. "From today on, I'm going to be the real me!" Then he added, "So why are you LOOKING FOR JUSTIN?"

You're right . . .

You are a sensitive artist!

Nicky filled Rob in on Justin's disappearance from NIAGARA FALLS and explained about their ongoing search. She even admitted how the friends thought that Rob might somehow be involved.

The captain of the THUNDER held up his paws. "Whoa. Not Me!" he protested. "I may like to give Justin a hard time about HOCKEY, but I would never do anything that crazy! I hope you find him!"

As Rob rejoined his father to work on the ice castle, the Thea Sisters waved good-bye.

"SEE YOU AT THE BIG GAME!"

BACK TO THE BEGINNING

Now that Rob had been ruled out as a suspect, the Thea Sisters headed back to Toronto. This case was getting more puzzling by the minute. Still, the mouselings had promised Adele and Liam they would help find Justin!

"We can't lose our focus," Paulina told the group after they had all gathered in Adele's living room. "We know Justin is okay because he called us. Now we just have to find out where he is!"

"And we need to find him soon," added Adele. "In two days, the coach will announce the new team captain! Justin has to be there!"

Together, the mouselings agreed to start from the beginning again.

"Let's talk to Justin's TEAMMATES," Violet suggested.

The next day, the Thea Sisters went to the ice rink to try to gather any small piece of useful information that might help them locate Justin. The questions were always the same: "How long has it been since you saw Justin?" and "Did Justin ever tell you he wanted to leave for a few days?"

We have to find him!

We won't quit!

Unfortunately, though, the *RESPONSES* they received were also always the same. No one had **SEEN** Justin since before the trip to Niagara Falls.

"I think that at this point we have spoken with everyone," said Violet, skimming the list of players that Liam had given them.

How long has it been since you saw Justin?

"No, look, one is missing . . . Elliott!" Pamela noted, *pointing* at a name that was not yet crossed out.

"He's that **PLAYER** down there," explained Paulina. "I remember because the coach is deciding between Elliott and Justin to be the new team captain."

"From what we've seen, he and Justin are **good friends**," added Nicky, feeling a **spark** of hope. "Maybe he will know something useful!"

The Thea Sisters waited for practice to finish and then climbed down from the stands and met Elliott at the exit to the rink. He seemed

When was the last time you saw Justin?

more than happy to help and remarkably remembered **everything** about the last time he had seen Justin.

Once the mouseling walked away, Nicky turned to Paulina. "What's wrong, Paulina? You have the strangest look on your face," she squeaked.

Paulina **FURROWED** her brow. "Maybe I'm wrong, but don't you think Elliott's responses were a little **TOO PERFECT**? I mean, think about it, we spoke with **tons** of players, and all of them had to think for a while before they answered our questions. And they even admitted that their memories might be a little **fuzzy**. But not Elliott."

"Of course! Why didn't we think of this before?!" exclaimed Violet suddenly. "Rob isn't the **only** one who would have an advantage if Justin weren't at the next game.

If Justin didn't show up, Elliott would **automatically** become the captain of the team!"

CLUE!
ELLIOTT AND JUSTIN BOTH WANT TO BE CAPTAIN OF THEIR HOCKEY TEAM, AND ELLIOTT HAD ALL THE PERFECT ANSWERS TO THE THEA SISTERS' QUESTIONS.

FRAMED BY A PHOTO!

Hoping they were finally on the right track, the Thea Sisters read over their clues. Elliott would have an enormouse *advantage* if Justin missed the big game. Was it possible that Elliott had something to do with his disappearance?

"Elliott? Are you sure?" exclaimed Liam when his friends **SHARED** their suspicions with him.

"We aren't sure," explained Pam.

"But we are convinced that we need to investigate further," Colette declared.

"The first thing we need to figure out is where Elliott was when Justin disappeared," advised Nicky.

"I've got it!" announced Liam, pulling out his laptop and logging on. It seemed that the Storms had created a special **blog**. On it, the players chatted about their days with their fans, posting **pictures** and funny sayings.

"There's a **photo** of you and Justin in Niagara Falls!" noted Paulina.

Liam nodded, "Yes, we uploaded it to show our fans that we were there on **vacation**."

Finally, the Thea Sisters felt like they were making progress on the case. Now if they could just find some photos posted by Elliott during the weekend Justin went **missing**!

Scrolling through all the photos posted by the players, the friends soon came across a few uploaded by Elliott. In one of the postings, he showed a **photo** of his breakfast. "The right meal to eat before

STORMS

MENU

THE
CHAMPIONSHIP
THE TEAM
PHOTO GALLERY
FACTS

CONTACT
WRITE US
ARCHIVE

 LIAM

PRACTICING
HARD FOR THE
GAME AGAINST
THE THUNDER!

Thursday

 ELLIOTT

THE RIGHT MEAL
TO EAT BEFORE
HITTING THE
BOOKS!

Saturday

 JUSTIN

EVEN HOCKEY
PLAYERS NEED A
LITTLE TIME OFF!

Saturday

HITTING the books!" Elliott had written.

"Oh well," sighed Nicky. "All this tells us is that our suspect was studying all weekend."

Paulina peered closely at the shot. Suddenly, she **smacked** her paw to her forehead. "Wait!" she squeaked excitedly, frantically scrolling through her own photos from her smartphone.

"I knew it!" she exclaimed finally, showing one of the photos to her friends. "**Do you notice anything strange?**"

The rodents looked at the two images.

"Oh, my goodmouse!" cried Colette. "The tablecloth and the PLATES and the

centerpiece are just like the ones in Niagara Falls!"

"Exactly," confirmed Paulina. "I'll bet you a **cheese donut** that Elliott wasn't home **STUDYING** like he wants us to believe. I'll bet he was in Niagara Falls!"

Tail twitching with anger, Liam punched in Elliott's number on his smartphone. "I'm getting to the **bottom** of this!" he insisted, turning on speakerphone so everyone could hear. But as soon as Liam mentioned Justin, Elliott said he had to go.

"Justin texted you that he was fine, so don't worry," he advised before hanging up.

I have to go . . .

Discouraged, Liam **STUFFED** his phone in his pocket, sinking into his chair with his snout in his paws. Now what? It seemed like every lead they had was ending up nowhere. The rest of the group felt just as dejected. Everyone, except for Paulina.

"Elliott is definitely involved," she insisted, explaining her theory to her friends. He pretended not to be in Niagara Falls. And Elliott had known about the **text message**, even though no one had mentioned a single word about it!

CLUES!

ELLIOT WAS IN NIAGARA FALLS AT THE SAME TIME AS JUSTIN AND THE THEA SISTERS. WHY DID HE TRY TO HIDE THAT?

A NEW CLUE

PUNChiNg Elliott's number into his cell phone, Liam wasn't surprised when this time it went right to **voice mail**. It was clear the mouseling was avoiding them.

"If he won't SQUEAK to us on the phone, we'll just have to squeak to him snout-to-snout!" suggested Pamela, pulling on her coat.

Where is he?

But Elliott was not in the campus **library** or at the **ice rink**.

So the group decided to try the **house** where he lived with his parents. Elliott's **mother** answered the door. "Liam, how nice to see you!" she exclaimed, recognizing her son's teammate.

After introducing his friends, Liam explained that they were looking for Elliott.

"I'm sorry, dears, but he went out for a **RUN** a while ago . . . You know, he wants

to be in SHAPE for the big game," Elliott's mom responded with a smile. "But I will tell him you came by."

The group thanked Elliott's mom and turned to leave right as Paulina noticed an **interesting** picture on the entryway table. It was a picture of the family in NIAGARA FALLS. "We were just there a few days ago," she commented, pointing to the photo.

Turning to look at the family picture, Elliott's mom beamed. "Oh, isn't it a **magical** place? We go often, since we have a cabin there," she explained.

The Thea Sisters, Adele, and Liam exchanged a look.

"Really?" Colette asked as a shiver ran down her fur. "And where is your cabin exactly?"

Happy to talk about a place she loved as much as warm cheese Danish, Elliott's mother gave the mouselings directions to the cabin. "Unfortunately, though, it's probably unreachable right now with the recent snowstorm," she commented, shaking her head. "The location is a little isolated, and the road to get there is closed."

Tamping down their excitement, the friends thanked Elliott's mom again, then scampered quickly to the car.

Without saying a word, everyone knew their next destination: Elliott's family's cabin! One way or another, they had to figure out a way to get there!

LIST OF IMPORTANT CLUES

1. THE TEXT MESSAGE THAT JUSTIN SENT DIDN'T SOUND LIKE HIM.

2. DURING THE CALL WITH JUSTIN, THERE WAS A LOT OF STATIC ON THE LINE.

3. ELLIOTT'S RESPONSES TO THE THEA SISTERS' QUESTIONS SEEMED REHEARSED.

4. ELLIOTT WAS IN NIAGARA FALLS RIGHT WHEN JUSTIN DISAPPEARED.

5. ELLIOTT KNEW ABOUT JUSTIN'S TEXT MESSAGE.

6. ELLIOTT'S FAMILY HAS A CABIN IN NIAGARA FALLS.

THE HIDDEN CABIN

Once again, the friends found themselves in the car driving toward NIAGARA FALLS.

While Liam drove CAUTIOUSLY on the snow-covered streets, Paulina used the satellite navigation on her TABLET to read out directions.

Make a right here.

"In eight hundred feet, you need to turn **right**," she announced.

"We haven't seen houses in a while," OBSERVED Violet from the back seat.

It was true. Just as Elliott's mom had described, the cabin

really was in the middle of *nowhere*!

"Elliott's mom said they call the cabin **Tunnel Retreat**," observed Colette. "I wonder why."

"Maybe you have to go through a **tunnel** to get there?" guessed Adele, pressing her nose against the GLASS and peering out.

Right then, Liam stopped the car. A metal barricade was set up in the middle of the road. **ROAD CLOSED** read a sign on the gate.

"Now what?" asked Colette, worried.

"Well, the road is closed to cars, not to pedestrians," noted Nicky, getting out of the SUV after Liam parked.

"Good idea," agreed Adele. "We have the SNOWSHOES we used when we went on that trip to the **Toronto Islands** in the trunk, and my parents' snowshoes are in there, too. Let's snowshoe!"

Strapping on the snowshoes, the friends began trekking carefully along a snowy trail. For a while, all they could hear was their own breathing and their soft pawsteps in the powdery snow.

"Uh-oh, I have bad news," Paulina announced as they rounded a corner. "I'm not getting any service in this area, so I can't use the navigator app."

Determined to find Justin, the group continued on in silence. But as they trudged **DEEPER** into the snowy **WILDERNESS**, the friends began to lose hope.

"Um, I hate to say it, but I feel like we're searching for a shaving of Parmesan in a giant bowl of spaghetti," Adele said, breaking the silence.

"If only we could find that tunnel," sighed Violet.

All of a sudden, Nicky stopped in her 🐾🐾🐾🐾🐾🐾. "Look!" she exclaimed. "The BRANCHES of those trees come together just like a natural tunnel!"

"Let's go!" exclaimed Paulina, hurrying down the path.

THE FAKE
EMERGENCY

As the friends rushed along, they could hardly contain their excitement. Were the trees really a natural tunnel or were they hurrying along to another dead end? It felt like forever, but at last the group reached the end of the trail and spotted a small WOODEN cabin.

"Justin!" Liam began to CALL, racing ahead. "Justin, are you here? It's us!"

Right then, the door to the cabin opened and Justin appeared.

"I KNEW YOU WOULD FIND ME!"

he squeaked happily.

The first to reach him was Adele. Relief at

finding her friend safe and sound **WASHED** away all feelings of shyness as she wrapped him in a **warm hug**.

"Oh, Justin!" the mouseling exclaimed. "I was so worried about you!"

"I'm okay, thanks," he reassured her, returning the hug. "And now that you're all here, I'm even better!"

Hurriedly **packing** up his belongings, Justin closed the door to the cabin and followed his friends to their car. Driving back to Toronto, Justin filled the group in on his wild adventure.

"I can't believe Elliott set a **TRAP** for me!" he said, shaking his head in disgust. "I realized the whole thing too late."

Justin explained that on the night of the **fireworks**, Elliott found him at the falls. "He told me there was some kind of

problem at his family's cabin. He asked me to lend him a  PAW, so I got my things and went with him. I figured I'd give you all a call later to let you know what happened."

"AND THEN WHAT HAPPENED?" the mouselets asked.

"Once we got to the cabin, I realized that

Come on!

there was no **EMERGENCY**. But before I could get to the bottom of things, Elliott said he had to get something from his car. A few minutes later, I heard the car **drive** off!"

"Cell phones don't work here . . ." observed Paulina.

"Yeah! When I tried to call you, I realized that Elliott had sent you a **text message** from my phone. He must have done it when we **STOPPED** to get gas on the way to the cabin."

Liam shook his head in **disbelief**.

Justin went on to explain how he had tried to call the group the next day, but at that point, his phone **battery** was dead and he had no charger. And with the **snowstorm** fast approaching, Justin decided the best thing to do was stay put and wait for things to **CLEAR** up.

"Plus, without the right equipment and directions, I knew it would be almost **impossible** to find my way out of the woods," Justin added.

"You did the right thing," Adele assured him as the rest of the group nodded in agreement.

After such an **ordeal**, the mouselings were sure Justin would want to relax at the dorm, but their friend had another idea.

"I need to make one **important** stop," he insisted.

LIAR, LIAR, FUR ON FIRE!

Meanwhile, over at the ice rink, the Storms zipped back and forth, warming up under the watchful EYE of their coach, Mr. Gerry Goalfur.

Coach Gerry was a MADMOUSE for the game of hockey. He loved everything about the sport, but most of all, he enjoyed watching his talented players grow together as a team. Running his eyes around the room, however, he realized that Justin, one of his most important players, was missing . . . again.

"Justin hasn't been to practice. And he hasn't **contacted** anyone," Elliott pointed out when the coach asked.

Disappointed in Justin's **irresponsible** behavior, Coach Gerry called a meeting. "Gather around, mice," he began. "I've made a decision about who will be our **new captain**. I must admit that I thought Justin would be my first pick, but the way he has behaved lately has caused me to **CHANGE** my mind. Therefore, our **new captain** will be —"

I have decided . . .

"Wait!" shrieked Nicky, interrupting Coach Gerry as she burst into the ice rink followed by the other Thea Sisters, Adele, Liam, and Justin. "Please, wait! Justin can explain!"

Shaking his head sadly, Coach Gerry walked slowly to the side of the rink. "So, Justin, you finally decided to join us. Unfortunately, I'm afraid it's too late," he announced.

Luckily for Justin, the Thea Sisters were there to jump to his defense. Together, they explained to the coach and the team exactly what had happened to Justin over the past few days.

"HE'S LYING!" exclaimed Elliott when they were finished, turning bright red. "I didn't mean to leave him at the cabin. I just forgot, I mean, I, um . . ."

Lies!

"You **FORGOT** you left your teammate alone in the middle of the **wilderness**?!" Coach Gerry said, staring hard at Elliott.

Elliott tried to protest, but Nicky interrupted him. "If I were you, I wouldn't tell any more **LIES**," she remarked. "You haven't told the truth in days, and we can **PROVE IT**!"

Quickly, the friends showed Coach Gerry the photos they had taken in NIAGARA FALLS and the pictures Elliott had posted on the team website.

"You published that photo on the team site to make everyone believe that you spent your weekend at home **STUDYING**," remarked Colette.

Finally, Coach Gerry had heard enough. After thanking the Thea Sisters for their wonderful **Detective** skills, he ordered Elliott off the ice. "I am afraid you will be kicked off the team for unsportsmouselike conduct," he squeaked.

Once Elliott had **slunk** out of the arena, Coach Gerry declared Justin the new **captain** of the Storms!

We'll see you tomorrow!

Welcome back!

A FURTASTIC GAME

Now that Justin was back, he was DETERMINED to catch up on all the practicing he had missed. The **BIG GAME** was only days away and he needed to get in shape.

Luckily, it was a lot easier to take *long* runs and practice complicated plays with his friends cheering him on.

On the day of the big game, a crowd of fans gathered in the

stands while the players **warmed** up. The Thea Sisters sat close to the **rink**.

"This hockey game is even more exciting than a trip to the **MALL**!" joked Colette, a self-described shopaholic.

Right then, down on the ice, the friends heard a familiar loud voice ring out. "Hey,

look who's here! Are you ready to **lose**?!" the voice challenged.

"Rob!" said Justin as the captain of the Thunder **SKATED** over to him.

"Oh no. Here we go again. I thought after we talked in Montreal he learned his **lesson** about being a **bully**," whispered Pamela.

But to everyone's surprise, at that moment, Rob **BURST** into laughter. "Don't get mad. I'm just joking," he said with a wide grin, **sticking** out his paw to shake Justin's. "I just came over so I could congratulate you on becoming **captain** and wish your team good luck. Here's to a **FURTASTIC** game!"

"Thanks!" Justin replied, matching Rob's smile.

"Come on, Storms!" squeaked Nicky when the official blew the whistle to signal the start of the game. For the next hour, the INTENSE match had the friends with their tails on the edge of their seats.

"I feel like I have whiplash!" joked Paulina, head swiveling back and forth as the

May the best team win!

players ZIPPED between the two goals on opposite sides of the ice.

Finally, in a *dramatic* finish, the Storms scored the winning goal with Justin leading the charge. Adele and the Thea Sisters jumped to their paws, clapping and cheering like a pack of riled-up rodents at a WILD WHISKERS concert.

"Justin was amazing!" Adele squeaked, eyes shining. "Did you see that last goal?"

The Thea Sisters grinned at one another. Even if Justin hadn't scored in the game, they knew he had already scored as a gentlemouse in Adele's eyes.

GOOD-BYE, TORONTO!

The next morning, the Thea Sisters prepared to return to **MOUSEFORD**. Their vacation in Canada had been so **fun**, they felt sad to say good-bye. Luckily, their flight was later in the day, so they had time for one more adventure in **Toronto**.

The suitcases are ready!

Before the friends could decide what to do, the doorbell rang. It was Justin.

"I know it's your friends' last day," the mouseling said, addressing Adele with a **warm** smile, "but I was wondering if you would like to take me on that **bird-watching** tour of the city. It sounded really interesting. We could all go!"

Bird-watching?

Well . . .

Of course!

Without realizing it, Adele let out an excited squeak. Instantly, her fur turned as red as a tomato. She had been trying for so long to ask Justin to go on the bird-watching tour and now he had beaten her to the punch!

"Um, w-w-w-ell, I — I — I —" she stammered, peeking shyly at the hockey player from beneath her lashes.

"What a fabumouse idea! She would love to go!" interrupted Colette, rushing to her friend's rescue. "And it's the perfect way to end our trip to Canada!"

So under a blue sky, the Thea Sisters and their new friends strolled along the winding trails in the heart of the city of Toronto.

"Hey, did you hear that?" whispered Nicky, stopping suddenly.

The friends strained their ears, and soon

they heard a pecking sound coming from a nearby tree.

"There he is! A woodpecker!" Pamela exclaimed under her breath, comparing the bird to a **SCARLET-HEADED** bird tapping at a tree in the Green Mouse brochure.

Everyone turned to look at the tree. Everyone that is . . . except for Colette.

"Hey, Coco, look, you're missing it. The **WOODPECKER** is over there . . ." Violet called to her.

"Mmmh," nodded Colette with a *funny* smile on her face.

Curious, the Thea Sisters followed their friend's gaze and slowly realized why she was smiling. It was Adele and Justin! The two were laughing and squeaking as they walked along paw in paw.

The five Thea Sisters exchanged happy

looks. Who would have guessed their trip to Canada would be so eventful? Besides solving the **mystery** of the missing mouse, the bird-watching tour was a fabumouse success!

"Now, those are my favorite kind of birds." Colette chuckled softly, nodding at Justin and Adele.

"LOVEBIRDS!"

Don't miss any of these exciting Thea Sisters adventures!

Thea Stilton and the Dragon's Code — **Thea Stilton and the Mountain of Fire** — **Thea Stilton and the Ghost of the Shipwreck** — **Thea Stilton and the Secret City** — **Thea Stilton and the Mystery in Paris**

Thea Stilton and the Cherry Blossom Adventure — **Thea Stilton and the Star Castaways** — **Thea Stilton: Big Trouble in the Big Apple** — **Thea Stilton and the Ice Treasure** — **Thea Stilton and the Secret of the Old Castle**

Thea Stilton and the Blue Scarab Hunt — **Thea Stilton and the Prince's Emerald** — **Thea Stilton and the Mystery on the Orient Express** — **Thea Stilton and the Dancing Shadows** — **Thea Stilton and the Legend of the Fire Flowers**

Thea Stilton and the Spanish Dance Mission — **Thea Stilton and the Journey to the Lion's Den** — **Thea Stilton and the Great Tulip Heist** — **Thea Stilton and the Chocolate Sabotage** — **Thea Stilton and the Missing Myth**

**Thea Stilton and the
Lost Letters**

**Thea Stilton and the
Tropical Treasure**

**Thea Stilton and the
Hollywood Hoax**

**Thea Stilton and the
Madagascar Madness**

**Thea Stilton and the
Frozen Fiasco**

**Thea Stilton and the
Venice Masquerade**

**Thea Stilton and the
Niagara Splash**

**Thea Stilton and the
Riddle of the Ruins**

And check out my fabumouse special editions!

THEA STILTON:
THE JOURNEY
TO ATLANTIS

THEA STILTON:
THE SECRET OF
THE FAIRIES

THEA STILTON:
THE SECRET OF
THE SNOW

THEA STILTON:
THE CLOUD
CASTLE

THEA STILTON:
THE TREASURE
OF THE SEA

THEA STILTON:
THE LAND OF
FLOWERS

THEA STILTON:
THE SECRET OF THE
CRYSTAL FAIRIES

Be sure to
read all my
fabumouse
adventures!

#1 Lost Treasure of
the Emerald Eye

#2 The Curse of the
Cheese Pyramid

#3 Cat and Mouse in a
Haunted House

#4 I'm Too Fond of
My Fur!

#5 Four Mice Deep in
the Jungle

#6 Paws Off,
Cheddarface!

#7 Red Pizzas for a
Blue Count

#8 Attack of the
Bandit Cats

#9 A Fabumouse
Vacation for Geronimo

#10 All Because of a
Cup of Coffee

#11 It's Halloween,
You 'Fraidy Mouse!

#12 Merry Christmas,
Geronimo!

#13 The Phantom of
the Subway

#14 The Temple of the
Ruby of Fire

#15 The Mona Mousa
Code

#16 A Cheese-Colored
Camper

#17 Watch Your
Whiskers, Stilton!

#18 Shipwreck on the
Pirate Islands

#19 My Name Is Stilton,
Geronimo Stilton

#20 Surf's Up,
Geronimo!

#21 The Wild, Wild
West

#22 The Secret
of Cacklefur Castle

A Christmas Tale

 #23 Valentine's Day Disaster

 #24 Field Trip to Niagara Falls

 #25 The Search for Sunken Treasure

 #26 The Mummy with No Name

 #27 The Christmas Toy Factory

 #28 Wedding Crasher

 #29 Down and Out Down Under

 #30 The Mouse Island Marathon

 #31 The Mysterious Cheese Thief

 Christmas Catastrophe

 #32 Valley of the Giant Skeletons

 #33 Geronimo and the Gold Medal Mystery

 #34 Geronimo Stilton, Secret Agent

 #35 A Very Merry Christmas

 #36 Geronimo's Valentine

 #37 The Race Across America

 #38 A Fabumouse School Adventure

 #39 Singing Sensation

 #40 The Karate Mouse

 #41 Mighty Mount Kilimanjaro

 #42 The Peculiar Pumpkin Thief

 #43 I'm Not a Supermouse!

 #44 The Giant Diamond Robbery

 #45 Save the White Whale!

 #46 The Haunted Castle

 #47 Run for the Hills, Geronimo!

 #48 The Mystery in Venice

 #49 The Way of the Samurai

 #50 This Hotel Is Haunted!

 #51 The Enormouse Pearl Heist

 #52 Mouse in Space!

 #53 Rumble in the Jungle

 #54 Get into Gear, Stilton!

 #55 The Golden Statue Plot

 #56 Flight of the Red Bandit

 #57 The Stinky Cheese Vacation

 #58 The Super Chef Contest

 #59 Welcome to Moldy Manor

 #60 The Treasure of Easter Island

 #61 Mouse House Hunter

 #62 Mouse Overboard!

 #63 The Cheese Experiment

 #64 Magical Mission

 #65 Bollywood Burglary

 #66 Operation: Secret Recipe

 #67 The Chocolate Chase

 #68 Cyber-Thief Showdown

 Up Next! #69 Hug a Tree, Geronimo

THANKS FOR READING,
AND GOOD-BYE UNTIL OUR
NEXT ADVENTURE!